Mystery at Heaven's Hill

To Emma,
Stay Sweet !!

Rebecca Iacobacci

Illustrated by Julian Regawa

Illustrated by Julian Regawa

Scripture quotations are taken from the Holy Bible, New Living Translation, copyright ©1996, 2004, 2015 by Tyndale House Foundation. Used by permission of Tyndale House Publishers, Inc., Carol Stream, Illinois 60188. All rights reserved.

WestBow Press books may be ordered through booksellers or by contacting:

WestBow Press
A Division of Thomas Nelson & Zondervan
1663 Liberty Drive
Bloomington, IN 47403
www.westbowpress.com
1 (866) 928-1240

ISBN: 978-1-9736-4184-1 (sc)
ISBN: 978-1-9736-4187-2 (e)

Library of Congress Control Number: 2018911821

Print information available on the last page.

WestBow Press rev. date: 10/09/2018

WESTBOW
PRESS®
A DIVISION OF THOMAS NELSON
& ZONDERVAN

This book is dedicated to God.
Thank you for giving me the gift of writing.
You are a faithful God!

It is also dedicated to
Carl, Debbie, Darla, and Shannette,
for pushing and encouraging me
to keep going forward.

Deep in the valley of Mount Tilly lays a quaint little town called Heaven's Hill. It isn't a very big town, but it is very well known. The people are friendly and loving in Heaven's Hill. They are kind to their neighbors, their friends, and their families. All the citizens of Heaven's Hill are different. Some are tall, some are short. Some have curly brown hair while others have straight hair as golden as the sun. Some of the people have very long names like Faith Anne Lynn Tullymoore. Others have short names like Jim Shore. But there is something more to Heaven's Hill. Something that makes the town and its people stand out like no other town. In fact, people come from miles around for this one thing.

The people in Heaven's Hill are very unique, but there is one thing that they all have in common. Everyone has the gift of cooking and baking! No matter what, they can all cook something. The best food they bake is pie. People from other towns and cities love to come to eat the delicious pies from Heaven's Hill. What kind of pies do they make, you might ask? Well, pick a pie, and they can make it! Blueberry, Apple, Banana Cream, Strawberry, Pumpkin, Peanut Butter and more. There are so many to choose from!

In the summer, Heaven's Hill has a special day when they celebrate this gift that God has given them; Celebration Day. On this day, everyone cooks one of their best meals or desserts and brings it to the giant festival. There is a parade filled with marching bands, horses, floats, and people throwing out candy to everyone. After the parade, they have a cookout with all the delicious food they prepared. They have the annual pie and watermelon eating contests and picnic games. In the evening, there is a concert followed by fireworks. The townspeople enjoy spending time with each other, and they take many pictures to capture all the fun.

One year on Celebration Day, everyone that was cooking and baking had their windows open. Heaven's Hill was beginning to smell wonderful! Garden Street smelled of blueberries, strawberries, and blackberries. Hedge Terrace smelled like pumpkin, sweet potatoes, and pecans. Faith Avenue smelled of chicken, hamburgers, hot dogs, and veggies slow roasting on grills. People walking down the streets were getting hungry because of all the delicious smells. They could not wait for the celebration to begin.

This year though, Celebration Day was different. The visitors for the festival were showing up early. The houses were all clean. Children were playing outside. The townspeople were gathering food and flowers from their gardens for the big feast. However, Heaven's Hill didn't seem quite right.

That morning, Hope Dey had just filled her pie crust with coconut cream filling. She placed the pie on the open windowsill in her kitchen for it to cool. Thirty minutes later she went to put it in the fridge, but to her surprise, the pie was gone!

"Now where did my pie go?" Hope thought to herself. "It didn't just walk away."

Hope looked out the window and down to the ground to see if her pie had somehow fallen. "Nope. It's not on the ground," Hope said to herself. "What happened to my Coconut Cream Pie?"

Down the road, George Zackery Michael Franklin was baking an apple pie. His kitchen window was open, and you could smell the sweetness of apples and cinnamon sugar. When the pie was finished, George put the apple pie on his windowsill. The summer breeze sent the delicious aroma down the street. George went about doing the rest of his morning chores, but when he returned to the kitchen, his pie was missing.

Over on Faith Avenue, Grandma Nettie was baking two of the best pumpkin pies she had ever made. Her grandchildren were outside playing in the yard, and they could smell the pies baking. The children were so excited and couldn't wait to eat them!

Grandma Nettie took the pies out of the oven, put them in her open window to cool off, and started cleaning up the kitchen. Meanwhile, her grandchildren decided they were going to put the final touches on their float for the parade.

"Grandma," called Lucy through the window.

Nettie came to the window. "Yes," she said.

"We are going to work on our float with our friends. Be back soon."

"Okay children, but be back by 12:30 so we can have lunch and then get ready to go to the parade," Grandma told them.

"Alright. See you later," the children chorused and ran off to finish their float.

Grandma Nettie left the kitchen and went about cleaning the rest of the house. When she returned to the kitchen a little while later, she discovered her wonderful pumpkin pies were gone!

"What could have happened to those pies?" She asked herself. "What am I going to do?" Grandma decided to pray. "Lord, you know what is going on and where those pies went. Please work this all out for your good. Thank you in advance for providing pies for the cookout later. In Jesus name, Amen."

Grandma Nettie went about her work and was trying to figure out some way to get another pie made. She was missing a couple ingredients to make a new one, so she decided to call her neighbor Lynn to see if she had sugar and eggs.

"Hello Lynn. This is Nettie. The strangest thing just happened. I put my pumpkin pies on the windowsill to cool and they disappeared! I'm missing some sugar and eggs to make a new one. Do you have any that I can use?"

"Yes, Nettie, I do," Lynn said. "It's interesting that you called because you aren't the only one this happened to. Hope and George had the same problem, along with some other people. Do you think the mayor knows about this?"

"I don't know, but I guess when we go to the parade later we will find out. Hopefully, the mystery will be solved. I'm coming to get the eggs and sugar. Thank you!" They hung up the phone. Grandma Nettie walked next door to get what she needed, then back home to bake another pie.

Grandma had just finished the new pie and started making grilled cheese sandwiches for her grandchildren when they all walked in the door.

"It smells so good in here!" they all exclaimed at once.

"Grandma Nettie, you make the best grilled cheese in the world!" exclaimed Lucy.

"Thank you, sweetie," Grandma said with a smile. "Now, how is the float coming? Is it all ready for the parade?"

"Yes! We are so excited. It is the best one there is!"

"Really? What is it going to be?"

"Oh, we can't tell. It's a surprise," said Lucy.

"Well, I can't wait to see your beautiful creation," Grandma told the children.

Grandma Nettie and the children finished lunch and got ready for the parade. They walked to the center of town to where all the action was. Grandma put her pie on a table under the dessert tent. The children ran off to the barn to get their float.

The citizens of Heaven's Hill and the visitors were lining up to watch the parade. People were sitting in lounge chairs and on blankets in the bright green grass along the side of the street. The mayor, Mr. Malachi Whitmore, was observing all the noise and excitement going on from the front steps of the town hall. Some of the adults had gone over to talk to him about all the missing pies. Mayor Whitmore reassured them that he would get to the bottom of it and all would be well. It was time for the parade to begin.

Mayor Malachi Whitmore marched to the middle of the street where there was a big red ribbon stretched out across the street to mark the start of the parade. The ends of the ribbon were held by two of the Kindergarteners from Heaven's Hill Elementary School. Mayor Whitmore took the microphone and began to address the crowd.

"Ladies and gentleman, thank you for coming out on this beautiful, summer day. We are here to celebrate all that God has done for us and given us. We are blessed that God has given us so many gifts and talents, which include baking and cooking. Before we begin, I want to mention something that has caught my attention. We all know how wonderful the town has been smelling today with all the food being made for later. It seems, though, that some of the pies made for the festival have gone missing from windowsills. This is a mystery that will be solved. We are looking into it and will sort it all out after the parade. So let's get going and start this party! Pastor Mike, please come and bless this day."

"Thank you, Mayor Whitmore. Let's pray. Lord, we thank you for this beautiful day you have given us. We thank you for all the wonderful gifts and talents you created us with. Please guide us each day as we use them to serve you and help others. We also ask that you give the mayor wisdom on the missing pie situation. We know that you know what is going on and we give the situation to you. Thank you for hearing our prayers and taking care of us. Bless this day of fun and keep everyone safe. In Jesus' Name, Amen."

After Pastor Mike finished praying the mayor cut the ribbon with giant scissors and the parade began. Heaven's Hill's fire trucks started the parade. They were blowing their sirens and had their lights flashing. Next came the Heaven's Hill High School Marching Band. They were wearing black uniforms that were outlined with purple stripes and had a large white 'H' on the front of their uniforms. People were driving old fashioned cars and horse-drawn carriages in the parade. The floats came in between the different bands, cars, and horses.

Each street made a float for the parade. The families on Hedge Terrace made their float to look like a garden of roses. The bottom of the float was green grass. They had a couple of palm trees on the float. It also had mini gardens that were filled with different colored roses such as red, pink, purple, white and yellow. There were mini rose bushes and four-foot tall bushes.

The next float had a backyard cookout theme. George Franklin was on the float with his grill cooking some hot dogs, hamburgers, and corn on the cob. It smelled so delicious! There were children playing catch with baseballs and gloves on the float as well. The backyard cookout float also had a picnic table and a small garden full of tulips, daffodils, and daisies.

The parade was so lovely, and everyone was having a great time. Clydesdale horses were at the end of the parade right before the last float. The horses were tall and different shades of brown. Some also had patches of white on them.

The last float was heading out onto the parade route. This float was the one everyone had been waiting for; it was the children's float. They called it Heaven's Hill's Best Pie. That it was too, for they had made their float into the shape of a giant pie! They were all inside it with the biggest smiles on their faces because they had a secret and it was about to be known.

As the great pie float went down the road, everyone cheered and took many pictures. It was round, and the outside was painted to look like a golden tan pie crust. The inside of the float had seats that the children could sit on. They were painted to look like different fruits that might go into a pie. The crowd noticed that the float also smelled like pies that had just come out of the oven. You could smell apple pie, sweet potato pie, pumpkin pie, and so many others. Everyone was impressed with this float, and they wondered how the children made the float smell so good. The answer to that question was soon to be revealed.

The Heaven's Hill's Best Pie float had a table in the middle of it and on that table were tons of pies. Both Grandma Nettie's and George Franklin's pies were there. So were Hope Dey's pie and about ten other pies that had gone missing earlier that morning. As the float went down the road, everyone began to notice their missing pies. No one was mad, but they were waiting to hear the explanation. When the pie float reached the park at the end of the parade route, Mayor Whitmore and Grandma Nettie were waiting to speak with the children.

"You have the best float of all," the Mayor said to the children. "And I think there is something that you need to tell everyone about your float. Lucy, do you want to tell us about it?"

"Ok," she said with a big smile. "We wanted our float to show off the town's uniqueness, which is our gift and ability to cook and bake. We are famous for our pies, so we decided to make the Heaven's Hill's Best Pie Float. What would make it the best? Pies, of course! Real pies. We made some of them but the rest we borrowed from windowsills today."

"Excuse me, Lucy," interrupted Grandma Nettie. "You said you borrowed them from the windows?"

"Yes," answered Lucy. "When someone made a pie on our street we would carefully look in the window to see if they were in the kitchen," Lucy explained. "We waited for them to go in a different room, grabbed the pie, put it in a wagon and rolled it away to the barn. We had them covered so no one would see them. Plus everyone was so busy getting ready for the day that people didn't pay much attention to children playing outside in yards."

"Lucy, did you ask to use the pies from the windows?" Grandma Nettie asked.

"Well, no. We wanted it to be a surprise," Lucy said.

"Lucy, you didn't ask permission to have the pies, and they don't belong to you. You thought that you were borrowing the pies because everyone would get them back after the parade, but really you were stealing them. Taking something that doesn't belong to you without permission is stealing. Do you children understand that and realize what you did was wrong?" Mayor Whitmore asked them all with love and softness in his voice.

"We didn't think of it like that. We would never steal. Our plan was that all the pies would go on the dessert table for the cookout after the parade," Lucy said with tears running down her face. "I know that stealing is wrong, we all do. We just wanted it to be a surprise. I am so sorry! Please forgive me for taking the pies without permission. Please forgive us," Lucy cried.

One by one, with tears streaming down their faces, all the children began to apologize for taking the pies. They realized what they did was wrong and that they should have asked first. After the children apologized, the Mayor, Grandma Nettie, and the children's parents gave all of them hugs.

"Children," said Mayor Whitmore, "We are not mad at you. What you did is wrong but I believe that you understand that now. I believe we all learned a great lesson here today. Lucy, would you like to finish telling us about the float?" The mayor asked.

As she wiped away her tears, Lucy started telling everyone about the float. "Well," she started. "We wanted to show that our town makes the best pies, not because of one person but because of everyone. No one can make a better pumpkin pie than my Grandma Nettie, just like no one can make a better apple pie than Mr. George Zackery Michael Franklin. We all work and bake together to help make this town special. So our float has everyone's pies in it."

"Thank you, Lucy," said Mayor Whitmore. "All of you children are wonderful and have reminded us of important things today. We were all reminded of how important it is to ask before taking something that doesn't belong to you. Lucy, you and your friends have also reminded us of how we need each other. You have shown us that when we put our gifts and talents that God has given us together, we can make something great. Nobody would want to go to a town where they only have one kind of pie. People want to go somewhere where they have a variety of pies. They would get tired of the same pie all the time. God has given us the ability to bless others with our gifts, and that is the reason why we are celebrating today."

"We realize now that taking the pies without asking was actually stealing and we will never do that again," Lucy told the Mayor.

"I'm glad you realize that," Said Mayor Whitmore. "Well, I believe that our pie mystery is solved! Thank you Lord for hearing our prayers and showing us what happened to the pies. In Jesus name, Amen. Now, who's hungry? Let's go have the cookout!" exclaimed the mayor.

Everyone in Heaven's Hill cheered. They went to the park and had a great cookout. There was so much food people didn't know what to eat first. But they made sure they left room for dessert!

There were activities for adults and children to play like bocce ball, a water balloon toss, and pony rides. There was face painting and a snow cone machine. People were talking about how lovely the parade was, how fun the cookout was, and how delicious all the food was. Adults and children alike went home with full tummies and smiles on their faces and in their hearts.

The people in Heaven's Hill truly enjoyed the day that started with a mystery and ended with a blessing.

1 Corinthians 12: 12 – 27 NLT

The human body has many parts, but the many parts make up one whole body. So it is with the body of Christ. Some of us are Jews, some are Gentiles, some are slaves, and some are free. But we have all been baptized into one body by one Spirit, and we all share the same Spirit.

Yes, the body has many different parts, not just one part. If the foot says, "I am not a part of the body because I am not a hand," that does not make it any less a part of the body. And if the ear says, "I am not part of the body because I am not an eye," would that make it any less a part of the body? [17] If the whole body were an eye, how would you hear? Or if your whole body were an ear, how would you smell anything?

But our bodies have many parts, and God has put each part just where he wants it. How strange a body would be if it had only one part! Yes, there are many parts, but only one body. The eye can never say to the hand, "I don't need you." The head can't say to the feet, "I don't need you."

In fact, some parts of the body that seem weakest and least important are actually the most necessary. And the parts we regard as less honorable are those we clothe with the greatest care. So we carefully protect those parts that should not be seen, while the more honorable parts do not require this special care. So God has put the body together such that extra honor and care are given to those parts that have less dignity. This makes for harmony among the members, so that all the members care for each other. If one part suffers, all the parts suffer with it, and if one part is honored, all the parts are glad.

All of you together are Christ's body, and each of you is a part of it.

CPSIA information can be obtained
at www.ICGtesting.com
Printed in the USA
BVHW02s2033191018
530729BV00005B/6/P

9 781973 641841